SeaBabies™

and their friends

by Cathleen Arone

Illustrated by Jack Crompton

World Leisure Corporation

Published by
World Leisure Corporation, P.O. Box 160,
Hampstead, New Hampshire 03841
Printed in Hong Kong

ISBN: 0-915009-56-0

Dear Reader:

Please allow me to introduce you to my friends, the SeaBabies — Sandy Dollar, Quahog Eddie, Herbie Fisher, Johnny Clam and Amy Plankton.

The SeaBabies have lived under the sea all of their lives. They're about to take us on a journey to their magical undersea world. Like our world above, it is a world of beauty and wonder, but even with the magic of the SeaBabies it is also a world threatened by pollution caused by carelessness and not thinking about other people.

Come and learn from the SeaBabies and the stories they tell us. Learn how we can make this a better world by working together and thinking about others.

Let's follow them as their adventure begins deep beneath the ocean blue.

Cathleen Arone
Author and President
SeaBabies, Inc.

Sandy Dollar

She is the leader of the family.
She is 12 years old, and full of energy and ideas. Sandy is very protective of her brothers and sister.

Quahog Eddie

(pronounced kwo-hog eddie)
Eddie looks up to his older sister.
He is 11 years old, has lots of common sense and is very thoughtful.
He is the big brother in the family.

Herbie Fisher

He is 8 years old.
Herbie is the serious and smart SeaBaby. He wants to be a scientist when he grows up.

Johnny Clam

He is 7 years old and full of mischief.
With Johnny around you know there will always be smiles and never a dull moment.

Amy Plankton

She is the little baby of the family.
She's only 5 years old and is sweet, shy and innocent.
She is very sensitive and loving.

One day, deep beneath the ocean waves,
Sandy Dollar and Quahog Eddie
were resting beside a coral reef.
Then their old friend, Mr. Larry Lobster, came clawing by.
He looked a little ill.

"Hello there!" exclaimed Sandy "My, you are looking rather blue today."

"I believe I'm coming down with the ocean flu," coughed Mr. Larry Lobster.

"Well, why don't you scuffle your way over to the ocean hospital?" suggested Sandy.

"I'm too weak," replied Larry.

"In that case, hop on my back. We'll take you to see Doctor Ollie Octopus," she said.

So Quahog Eddie and Sandy Dollar swam away with Mr. Larry Lobster toward the ocean hospital to see if Doctor Ollie Octopus could help.

"Oh Doctor Octopus," cried Sandy Dollar
and Quahog Eddie,
"you must help our friend.
He is not feeling well."

Doctor Ollie Octopus
got out his thermometer
and stethescope.
He began to examine
Mr. Larry Lobster.
"Ah-ha . . . um-hum," the doctor
sighed after a brief check-up.
"Just what I thought.

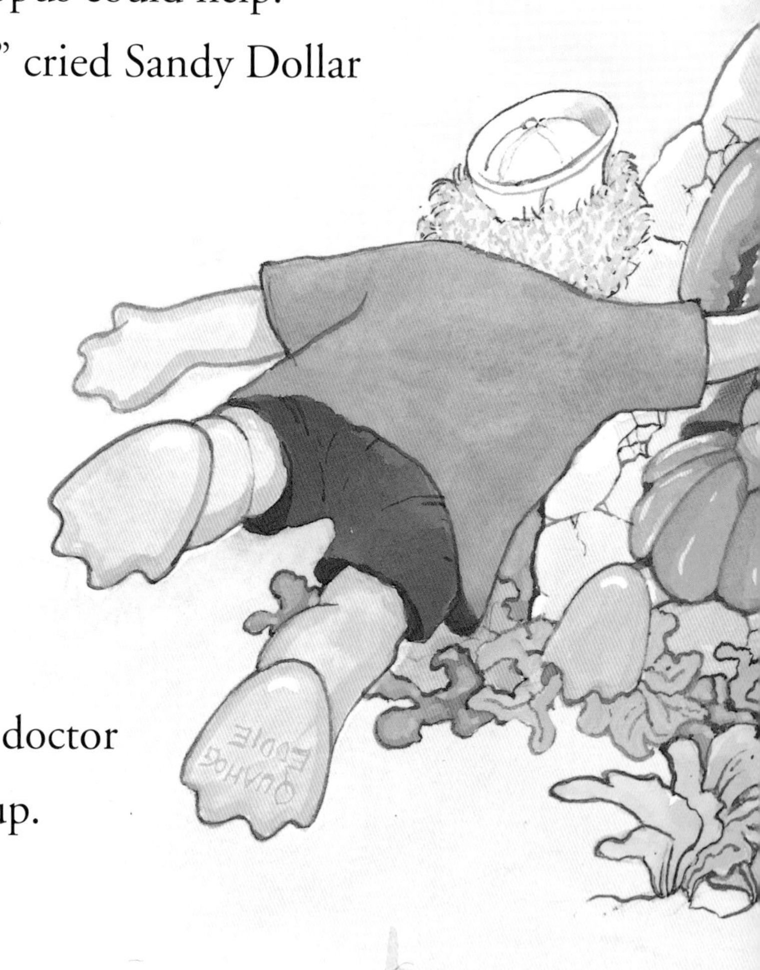

I'm afraid our dear Mr. Larry Lobster has come down with a case of the ocean flu.
We've been seeing an awful lot of that lately.
He'll need to be treated with some oceanbiotics!"

"Oh no," Sandy gasped, "this ocean flu is making all our undersea friends sick."

"Just what is this ocean flu? Where did it come from?" she wanted to know.

"And why are we getting it?" questioned Quahog Eddie.

The good doctor gave an understanding glance.

"Well, my friends, the flu is caused by something called pollution from the people living on the land," he said.

"Doctor Ollie," Sandy called as she scrunched up her seashell nose and scratched her seaweed hair, "I don't understand. What's pollution?"

Doctor Ollie looked at them both. "We call it pollution when land people make the water we live in dirty by throwing away things they don't need anymore like empty bottles, pens that won't write, paper cups and old tires.

They think it disappears but we know it doesn't."

Sandy Dollar hugged her brother. She asked, "Don't land people like us? Why would they want to make us sick?"

"They don't do it to hurt us," Doctor Ollie answered, "They don't even think about us. They just do it because they are thoughtless and because it is easier for them."

He waved his arms to make his point and continued, "There are many little things they do that are easier for them but make it harder and harder for us to live healthy lives at the bottom of the sea.

"The problem is only getting worse. There is simply nothing that we can do about it," the doctor sighed.

Quahog Eddie and Sandy Dollar looked at each other. "We've got to do something!" they both said.

"We must go back to our sand castle home and talk about this problem with our brothers and sister," said Eddie. "Maybe together we can find a way to make things better."

With that the SeaBabies said goodbye to the doctor and the lobster.

They swam away swiftly toward their undersea sand castle home. Along the way they found a sunken ship on the ocean floor.

"Quahog Eddie . . . let's stop here and take a look inside," exclaimed Sandy. "We know very little about the land people. Maybe there is something inside this ship that will help us learn about land people."

"Great idea!" agreed Eddie.

"Maybe we can find something to help us understand what is happening!"

"Wow! This ship is filled with all kinds of things!" exclaimed Quahog Eddie as he began to sift through a stack of books.

"Look at this, Sandy," he said as Sandy Dollar came to his side.

"Great! There are so many different kinds of books," Sandy said. "We'll learn something about land people by reading these books."

“This book has pictures of the stuff that has been dumped on us!” said Quahog Eddie.

“All those strange-looking things are here . . .
tires, oil cans, gasoline,
soda cans . . . and shoes!”

“Let’s take these books back with us to our sand castle,” said Sandy Dollar.

“Take as many as your little webbed hands will carry!”

The SeaBabies filled their arms with books and swam off.

SANDY
DOLLAR

When the SeaBabies returned to their castle home Sandy Dollar called for a family meeting. Everyone was there — Sandy Dollar, Quahog Eddie, Herbie Fisher, Johnny Clam and Amy Plankton.

They all sat and listened to their big sister, Sandy.

"Our world is being infected by the ocean flu! We have learned from Doctor Ollie Octopus that the flu is caused by what land people are doing up above us.

When they throw things away into the ocean it is called pollution," began Sandy Dollar.

"Quahog Eddie and I have brought back books from the sunken ship so that together we may learn more about the land people and the pollution that is causing our ocean flu."

The SeaBabies family then began reading through the books from the sunken ship.

Herbie Fisher pushed his glasses up on his nose as he read.

"Wow!" he shouted. "These land people put all kinds of things in our ocean."

"What is that?" asked Amy Plankton, pointing to a picture in her book with her webbed hand.

"Let's see," said Herbie Fisher as he carefully studied the picture Amy had pointed out. "There are cola cans, plastic bags, old pills, pieces of soap . . . Yuck."

Sandy was upset. "No wonder our friends are getting sick," she said.

"Look at this picture!" shouted Johnny Clam. "The land people look a lot like us . . . only we have webbed hands and feet, a seashell nose and seaweed hair."

"They don't look like they want to hurt us," said Quahog Eddie.

“I think that Quahog Eddie and I should swim up to the ocean surface and look around,” suggested Sandy Dollar. “We need to find out more about what is causing the ocean flu. If we don't do something soon, everyone will be sick!”

Sandy Dollar and Quahog Eddie then left for the unknown and completely unexplored ocean surface!

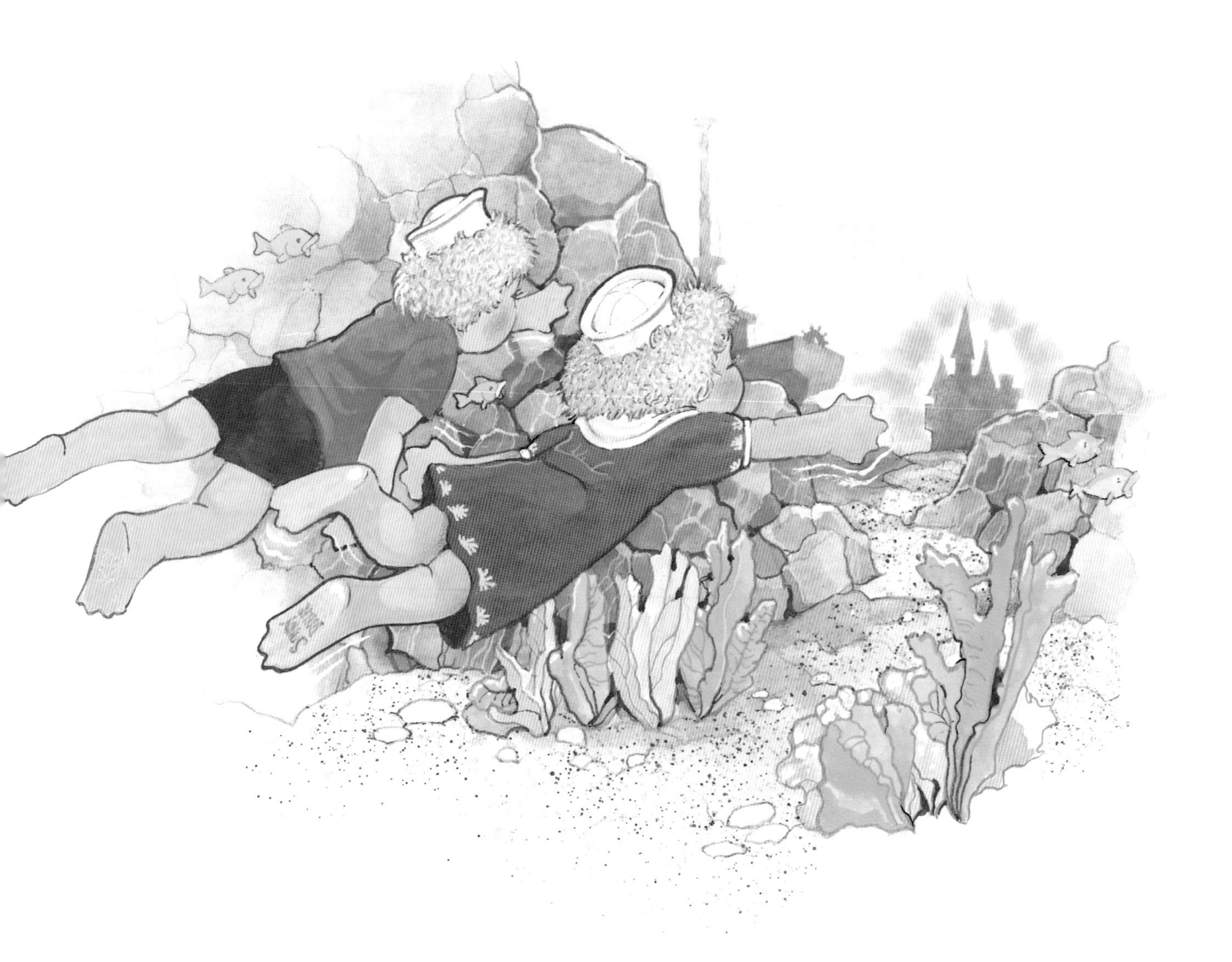

As they swam up to the surface of the ocean, the sunlight made everything brighter and they saw things they had never noticed before. They found an old grocery bag, a tennis shoe, a cleaning rag and a paper cup floating just below the ocean surface.

"What's this stinky and sticky stuff?" Sandy Dollar groaned when they arrived at the surface.

"I'll never get it out of my seaweed hair and it really smells."

"Look! Over there is a boat with land people on it," exclaimed Eddie motioning to Sandy. "Do they look friendly?"

Only a short distance away there was a boat with three men working on it.

Sandy Dollar wiped her eyes.
"Yes Eddie, they might be friendly,
but look what they're doing!"
Sandy said in horror.
"Shhhhh . . . listen!"

"Okay men," the captain said,
"this looks like as good a spot as any.
Let's get started and move fast.
Gotta dump this toxic junk
while no one's around . . .
don't want to get caught!"

The SeaBabies watched
in shock as the men began
to dump messy and gunky stuff from
the containers into the water!

CAUTION

They had never seen anything like this before. The goo spread slowly toward them and they backed away kicking their webbed feet furiously.

Sandy Dollar and Quahog Eddie's eyes began to sting and their seashell noses began to burn.

"Let's get out of here!" cried Eddie. "I can't even breathe. I want to go home."

"So this must be why our friends are catching ocean flu," said Sandy Dollar. "This must be one of the bad things Doctor Ollie Octopus told us about. Let's go see him right away!"

"How can land people do such a horrible thing?" Quahog Eddie asked with tears in his eyes. "I feel sick."

"What else are they dumping on top of us?"

"I don't know Eddie, but cover your seashell nose quickly and let's go," cried Sandy Dollar.

Sandy Dollar and Quahog Eddie swam swiftly to the ocean hospital.

"Doctor Ollie! Doctor Ollie Octopus! We saw the land people dumping something stinky and sticky they called toxic junk into our oceans," Sandy Dollar said sadly. "It made our eyes sting and it smelled so bad we couldn't stand it."

"What can we do?" asked Quahog Eddie.

Slowly, the doctor replied, "My dear SeaBaby friends, this is one of many reasons that our friends in the ocean are becoming sick."

"Please doctor, we can't just give up!" begged Quahog Eddie.

"We will never give up!" promised Sandy Dollar.

They quickly swam back to their castle. When all the Seababies were together, Quahog Eddie began, "Brothers and sisters . . . we must tell you what we have discovered. Our kingdom is in great danger because of the pollution that is being dumped on us by the land people."

The rest of the SeaBabies looked confused.

"What can we do?" asked Johnny Clam.

"Maybe we can find some way to tell the land people how sick they are making us," suggested Quahog Eddie.

Amy Plankton held up her favorite picture from the books and said, "Land people don't look mean."

"Is it too late? Can we clean up the pollution?" questioned Herbie Fisher.

"It's never too late!" shouted Sandy Dollar. "We'll never resolve any problem if we don't work together to make this a better world."

Johnny Clam, who was sitting down and thinking hard, asked, "How come we never get sick?"

"That's right! Why?" the others asked.

Sandy Dollar said, "I believe that since our sand castle was built so well and so long ago, it must have protected us from the pollution. The pollutants simply can't get in here.

That is why it is magical.

That must be why we are healthy!"

Quahog Eddie jumped up. "I have an idea," he announced.

“Why don’t we move Doctor Ollie Octopus and hispatients here to our magic castle? That way they will be protected from the pollution and they’ll feel better!”

“Good thinking,” said Herbie Fisher and Johnny Clam. Amy smiled and clapped her hands.

"But this is a problem that involves all of us.
Let's have a Sea-Call to invite all our friends.
By sharing the problem, we have more power to
find ways to keep our ocean world clean
and to keep us all healthy," Sandy Dollar stated.

"Working together, we can find the answers.
Maybe we can find a way to tell land people
how much their carelessness hurts us."

"That's a great idea," answered Herbie Fisher.

"Yes . . . team effort!" said all the SeaBabies as they began planning to save their undersea world.

"OK, let's get to work. Nothing will change until we start," said Sandy Dollar. "With everyone working together, we can and will make a difference!"

The SeaBabies turned to all their friends and said together, "Tell everyone you meet that they can help, too. Every little thing anyone can do makes a big difference."

For more information about SeaBabies and how everyone can help keep our oceans clean send a card or letter to: SeaBabies, Inc., P.O. Box 2641, Orleans, MA 02653
SeaBabies can be found on the internet at http://www.seababies.com
A portion of this book's profits will be donated to efforts of environmental responsibility.